LITTLE MISS HUG

HUG

originated by Roger Hargreaves

Written and illustrated by Adam Hargreaves

Grosset & Dunlap
An Imprint of Penguin Random House

Have you ever fallen over and hurt yourself?

I bet you have.

And then, have you wished that someone would come along to give you a hug and make you feel better?

Well, Little Miss Hug is just that person.

Like the time she found Little Miss Tiny after she had fallen off the curb.

But there is something else extra-special about Little Miss Hug's hugs.

It is her extra-special arms.

They fit perfectly around whoever she is hugging.

Whether it is Mr. Small after a twig falls on him and squashes his hat . . .

. . . or Mr. Bump after one of his bumps.

Or even Mr. Greedy when he has a tummy ache.

Little Miss Hug is always there with a perfectly fitting hug to make everything better.

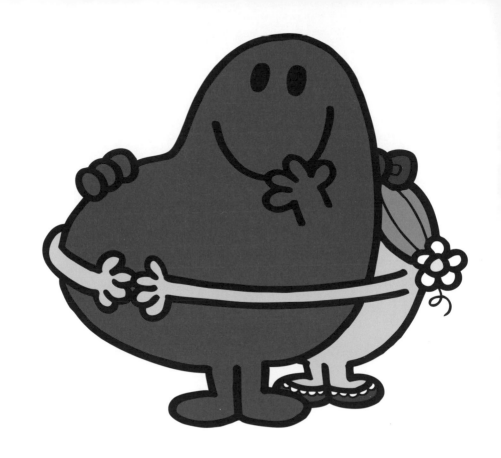

Then there are times when nobody has hurt themselves.

Happy times like birthdays.

Everyone wants a birthday hug!

And times when Little Miss Hug hugs someone just for the fun of it.

Even someone like Little Miss Bossy needs a hug once in a while.

Everyone needs a hug.

Or so Little Miss Hug thought.

The other day when she was out for a walk, she heard someone hiding on the other side of some bushes.

Someone huffing and puffing and moaning and groaning.

Someone who was in a very bad mood.

It was Mr. Grumpy!

And why was Mr. Grumpy in such a bad mood?

Because the sun was out!

There really is no pleasing Mr. Grumpy.

Quick as a flash, Little Miss Hug ran around the bushes, stretched out her arms, and hugged Mr. Grumpy.

Or at least she tried to, but something happened that had never happened to Little Miss Hug before.

Mr. Grumpy pushed her away.

"Get off me!" shouted Mr. Grumpy.

Little Miss Hug could not believe her ears.

She could not believe her eyes.

Nobody had ever refused one of her hugs!

"But . . . but, everyone likes a hug!" she cried.

She was so confused she hugged Mr. Grumpy again.

"I know what you are trying to do," said Mr. Grumpy. "But it won't work. I am grumpy, and I like being grumpy. No amount of hugging will change that."

Little Miss Hug didn't let go.

"I said . . ." began Mr. Grumpy. But then he stopped.

Something was happening to Mr. Grumpy that had never happened to him before.

He could feel a strange, warm feeling spreading out from deep inside him.

Little Miss Hug hugged him tighter.

And then the most extraordinary thing happened.

Very slowly, Mr. Grumpy smiled.

For the first time in his life, he was happy.

Little Miss Hug let go of him.

"I must say," said Little Miss Hug. "You have a lovely smile."

And can you guess what Mr. Grumpy did next?

He blushed!

For the first time in his life, he blushed.

And then he hugged Little Miss Hug.

For the first time in his life, he hugged someone!

Although, as you can see, it was an almost-hug, not a proper Little-Miss-Hug hug.

What you might call . . .

. . . half a hug!

A Mr. Grumpy hug.

And that was a great start.